"GO

That was most often in those hills a warning yelled to a lawman by someone who didn't want to kill him but damn sure would if he failed to heed the warning.

"That son of a bitch," said Foster.

"Hey," I shouted. "Henry. It's Charlie. Foster just wants to ask you a couple of questions. It's okay, Henry. He even let me ride out here with him. Come on outside."

"Go back."

I recognized old Malachi's voice that time. Then Mose stepped out the door of the cabin, leaving it open.

"Hey, Foster," he called. "You going to take Henry in?"

"I ain't here to take nobody in. Not just yet. I just got some questions for him about them two boys that's killed."

Henry stepped out and kind of pushed Mose aside, stepping in front of him. He was holding his rifle.

"Oh God, no," I said, just barely out loud.

"How do I know that, lawman?" yelled Henry.

Foster spoke to me. "Them bastards is looking for a fight," he said.

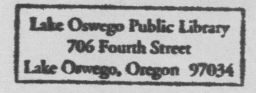

BACK TO MALACHI

ROBERT J. CONLEY

LEISURE BOOKS **NEW YORK CITY**

All of the characters in this book are fictitious,
and any resemblance to actual persons, living or dead,
is purely coincidental.

A LEISURE BOOK®

July 1997

Published by

Dorchester Publishing Co., Inc.
276 Fifth Avenue
New York, NY 10001

Printed in the United States of America.

for
Clu Gulager,
for
Don Coldsmith,
and for
Vicki Snell

AUTHOR'S NOTE

Some years ago while attempting research into the life of Ned Christie, I again ran across one of those references from a prominent "six-gun historian" (the phrase is Emmet Starr's) which said, in effect, that Ned Christie, a full-blood Cherokee, was the worst outlaw ever to roam the Indian territory. That is a bold statement. I tried in vain to find evidence to substantiate that claim. What I found were references to other "bad Cherokee outlaws," equally unsubstantiated. I have since, following further research and cogitation, written an article for *The Roundup*, "Cherokees 'On the Scout,' " which is an investigation of this phenomenon. In the meantime, I wrote *Back to Malachi* as a fictional exploration of the topic. Mose Pathkiller is not Ned Christie, though there are some similarities between the two and the manner of his death is an almost direct borrowing from the Ned Christie story.